JN273719

黒い波

ドラゴ・シュタンブク詩集

橋本博美 訳

思潮社

BLACK WAVE by TOMISLAV BUNTAK   TOKYO 2008

黒い波　ドラゴ・シュタンブク詩集　目次

深き紅の歌　8

黒い波　12

一九一八年　16

隠者　18

ドラゴンの島　20

ヨナ　22

寄り道　24

ブラック・ウィドウ　28

わが父は聖域(サンクチュアリ)を満たしたもう　30

手首　34

荒涼の山並み、シナモンの香り　38

言葉の刃　40

ベンガルの美しき女　42

レイモンド・カーヴァーの指輪　46

環　50

クレオパトラの毒蛇（メテムシコーシス） 52
輪廻転生 54
絶壁 56
夜のガスパール 58
ハート型の魚 60
天の底（ナディール） 62
ターニング・ポイント 64
ZEPHYR（そよかぜ） 66
日本の絵はがき 68
ドラゴ・シュタンブクのこと　テス・ギャラガー 70
謝辞 77
著者略歴 79

後援　ユナイテッド　オーシャン　エンタープライズ　株式会社

黒い波

深き紅の歌

夜啼く鳥よ、夜啼く鳥よ、おまえの気高き心(ハート)はどこに宿るのだろう

バラの棘の上、
バラの棘の上だよ。

夜啼く鳥よ、夜啼く鳥よ、おまえの鼓動(ハート)はどこで脈打つのだろう

愛しいひとの窓の傍、
愛するひとの窓の傍だよ。

夜啼く鳥よ、夜啼く鳥よ、おまえの心臓(ハート)が血を流すのはどこ

バラの棘の上、
バラの棘の上だよ。

夜啼く鳥よ、夜啼く鳥よ、その血はどこへ流れてゆくの

バラの紅(くれない)の中、
バラの紅(くれない)の中だよ。

夜啼く鳥よ、夜啼く鳥よ、おまえの傷口から滴る血の匂いを嗅ぐのは誰

群青の海からやって来る　わたしの愛しいひと、
紺碧の空からやって来る　ぼくの愛するひとだよ。

夜啼く鳥よ、夜啼く鳥よ、おまえは夜、空を飛ぶのか
それとも　もの悲しげに夜想曲(ノクターン)を唄うのだろうか

飛びもしない、唄いもしない
ただ血の滴(したたり)に耳を澄ませるだけ。
ぽたり　ぽたり
ただ深き紅の行方を見守るだけ。

黒い波

あなたの愛になりたい
あなたの艱難辛苦となりたい
あなたの顔となり
あなたの突き刺すような寒さともなろう
あなたの炎になりたい
あなたの海に突き出た断崖となりたい
あなたのために狂おしく猛進し
あなたのために鋭いきっ先ともなろう

あなたの歌になりたい
あなたのあらゆる痛みになりたい
あなたの海となり
あなたの唯一の神ともなろう
あなたの銀の盃ともなろう
あなたの瞳となり
あなたの砂丘になりたい
あなたの影になりたい
あなたの名前となろう
あなたの心　あなたの夢となり
わたしは青い船になって
揺れながらともに　海原を渡ってゆくだろう

それから　わたしはあなたの島になろう
あなたの家の入口となり　あなたのワインになる
あなたの揺りかご　あなたの土地
あなたが受け継いだもの　そして恐怖
あなたが焦がれるすべてのものになろう
たとえそれが見果てぬ夢であっても
急降下　垂直上昇
無限　白銀の頂き　金色(こんじき)の果て
あなたが望むあらゆるものに　わたしはなってみせよう
たとえこの身の破滅とわかっていても
ただ一つだけ　なりたくないのは？
あの黒い波に　奪い去られるもの

一九九五年一月、ニューデリーにて

一九一八年

帆船が群れをなして往く
遠い異国の地へ
わたしたちの愛しいひとを連れ去って
帆船は群れをなして往く　遙か彼方へと
積荷には真白い小麦粉
黄金色の油の樽　そして
わたしたちの命も詰めこんで
強欲な異国の地へと奪い去ってゆく

帆船は群れをなして往く　遙か彼方へと
舳先で引き裂かれる心と心
ああ　どうしたらよいのか
遠い異国へ去って往く　わが分身たちよ

隠者

かくして　わたしたちは金の環の中で
久遠の日々を生きている

すべては環の中　堪え忍ぶ愛
絡み合う思考　結ばれた思慕

山羊革のカバー　聖杯　炎

始まりと終わりが
円を描いて繋がる

指環の芯で　ぬらぬらとしたぬくもりが
せわしげに渦巻く
あなたの骨張った指で　それは脈打っている

ドラゴンの島

オンブレッタ・デ・スタンブッコのために

今宵　雲は月を貪り、その紫色の指で
銀色に輝く月の面(おもて)をかき砕く
やがて　この不完全な世界の果てで
幾重にも重なる物憂い暈から浮かび上がった
神聖なる月が
被毛の焼け焦げた狼たちによって引き裂かれるとき
合金の煌く光がブラチ島の頂に降り注ぎ
闇にうごめく獣どもの足跡を　いまわの際のざわめきに変える。

訳注　ブラチ島はクロアチアにある著者の生まれ故郷の島。

一九八三年八月　セルカにて

ヨナ

船の腹の中でうたた寝しているうちに
わたしたちは嵐に流され
深い海へと葬られてしまうだろう

いったいこの嵐はどこから来たのか
わが命の果てが　なぜこうなるのかも
知らぬままに

絶望の中で　わたしは問い掛ける
われわれは　どんな夢を見るのだろうかと
荒れ狂う風が　わたしたちを　深く　深く

暗い海の激流の底へと引き込んでゆくというのに

訳注 ヨナはヘブライの預言者。神の命に背き船で逃亡しようとするが、嵐に見舞われその責めを負い海に捨てられたところを大魚に呑み込まれる。旧約聖書「ヨナ書」参照。

寄り道

かたく閉じた窓辺に佇んで
ひとり　見つめているひと。

ひび割れた窓枠から
風が吹き込み
厚いカーテンを揺らす。

そのひとが見つめているのは
人けのない広場
端から端へと紙袋が風に舞う。

時計はとうの昔に三時を告げた。
たぶん　彼は
本屋の店先で立ち読みをしているのかしら。
ひどく寒がり屋の彼のことだから
肌を刺す突風に吹かれたら大急ぎで飛んでくるはず。
たぶん　引き留めたのは彼のお母さん、それとも
不意の仕事、焼き餅を焼いた恋人・・・。
彼女は午後のあいだずっと　そんなふうに彼を待っていた、
この屋根裏部屋で。
吐息が窓枠やガラスに凍りついてしまった。

暗くなりはじめたマルル広場に灯りがともる。
冬が吠える。
そして彼女は　あいかわらず
窓のそばで佇み
ひとり　待ちつづけている。

　　　　　　　　　　　　一九八六年十二月　スプリトの街で

訳注　マルル広場は、クロアチア・スプリト市の中心にある広場

ブラック・ウィドウ

ブラチ島で毒蜘蛛を見た。ブラック・ウィドウ生物学教授ドミニク・ブラヒニッチが捕まえてガラス容器に入れておいた奴だ。
黒く長い足、赤い斑点のある黒々とした背中、黒い頭、そして餌食となった獲物の体に毒を注入するための　黒く長いきょう角
こいつがもし枕の下にいたらと　想像しただけで体が震えた。
恐怖に顔は黒ずみ、引きつった唇は海豚の口さながら。
アドリアの海が千個あってもあのおぞましい感覚を薄められはしまい。

詩は海の泡。蜘蛛は風下に棲む
だが　黒い背中に赤い斑点のあるブラック・ウィドウは
天上に君臨する。
その美しさは不可解にして、いかなる壮麗な天使よりも手強い。
神こそわが証人である。あのガラス容器を眼前にしたとき
私はただ　深く悔いた　ちっぽけな罪人だった。
私は露を含んだ木の端くれ、星々の木立の中にこぼれたひとかけら。

　　　　　　　　　　　　　　　　　一九八七年

わが父は聖(サンクチュアリ)域を満たしたもう

青き果実を摘むことなかれ
熟れるがままにまかせよ。
蒔いた種には
忍耐をもって臨むべし。

わが息子、わが神。

木は己が身を食べず
川は己が水を飲まぬ。
剣は子どもの手に委ねるためにあらず

ペンは戦士の拳のためにあらず。

わが息子、わが神。

死とは己が家へ
帰還することなり。

命　芽生えるところ
すでにして闇の住処なり。

わが息子、わが神。

言葉は汝が心に潜め
己が体を振り払い、うち捨てよ。
道半ばにて自らを見失い
かき消さるることなかれ。

砂を融かし、黄金を産ましめよ。

わが息子、わが神。

有効期限の無きものなり。
慈悲は　小瓶に入りし
そは己れの内に見つけ、正すべし。
他人の不徳を探すことなかれ。

わが息子、わが神。

真実を知りたいと欲するなら
暴かねばならぬ。
我らが目に　主は現れる。
我らは大海の名残りをとどめる一滴なり。

わが息子、わが神。
良きことを思い、良きことを為せ。
他者の魂のなかに
己が魂を見いだす者よ、
汝は神となるであろう。

手首

カフェ・ハーグで　私はコーヒーを飲まなかった
ボスニア出身のムハッメドが
おずおずと差し出したのは
掌でなく　手首
手は
石灰で汚れているから　と。

彼の仕事場は
ダヴィンチの創作展示場に隣接したベネディクト修道院
人間の心を浄め、想像力を鍛えてくれる場所だ

ゆっくりとしたボスニア流の足運びと
よれよれの作業着を見て、私はすぐに同郷の民と分かった
白い粉にまみれたその姿は
さながら労働者の天使。

私は差し出された手首を握る
が、すぐに
彼の白くなった掌を取り直し
握手しながら 言った
「神聖な手だ」。

彼は不調法を詫びる
カフェ・ハーグでコーヒーなんか啜ってるのを見つかったら
ボスに大目玉を食らっちまうんで

彼はルドの生まれで、妻はサラエボの出身
ハミダとベンヤミン、二人の子供がいる
年は三十五歳というが、それよりずっと老けて見えた
わたしたちが交わすことのできた会話は　それだけ。

ウィーンの真ん中で出会った
ボスニアの真ん中出身のムハメドとの　これが一期一会
粉まみれの手　粉まみれの作業着で
握手のために、手首を差し出したムハメド
繊細な青白い肌は、その部分だけが
モルタルの粉で汚れることもなく
脈が取れそうにくっきりと　静脈が透けて見えた
その下を、とくとくと脈打っていた命の血潮。

カフェ・ハーグの口を付けなかったコーヒーと
幼な子の顔のように白い手首は
地の果てまでも　私に付いて廻るだろう
彼の手首と優しさゆえに、あのぎこちない歩き方ゆえに
ボスニア、愛深き心
おのれの一番奥底の　一番優しいものを捧げる
天使の肌を持つ人々。

二〇〇五年三月十一日　ウィーン、ショッテンガッセ通りにて

荒涼の山並み、シナモンの香り

荒れ狂う言葉の海を渡りきった果てに
われわれの心にもたらされたのは　ガラスの静寂だった。
(海も山も)　一目ですべてをこの眼に取り込み
白く燃えさかる小さな点に凝縮するのだ
おのれの　そして他人の
あらゆる心を　魔法の絨毯に包み込んで
山々へ　たなびく雲へ　山上に庵る人々のもとへ
そうして彼らの寺院へと　運んでゆこう。

言葉の刃

偶然に投げかけられた一つの言葉に突き刺され、
私は記憶の傷跡に逃げ込んだ。
体を丸め　捩り　四方八方からくるまれる。
テーブルの上に積み上げた　母のリネンのテーブルクロスみたいに。
そうして　ぴったりと合わさった脳の襞の奥に　身を隠した。

チェックの国旗に身を包んだまま
私は今もなお　北風に身を開くこともない。
われわれは　賭けに負けたのだ。千と一つの機会をすべて失ってしまった。
代わりに築き上げたのは　もめ事の絶えぬ家、溜息の尽きぬ国

そこは　究極の隘路　大海の一滴に溢れる空隙。

そしてあなたときたら　にやりと笑い　真四角な都市都市から熟れた林檎を空へ向かって放り上げるというのか　ああ　まるで虫けらのように。

チェックメイト　それは　取るに足らない幸福の理由
開いた扉を開けるための鍵。

ベンガルの美しき女

ベンガルの美しき女(ひと)よ、
通りすがりの旅人に饗する
一杯の紅茶のために
あなたがその乳房から乳を搾ったとき
哀しみが私を押し潰した。

帰国すれば皆が　私に尋ねるにちがいない
ひとの乳が入った紅茶とはどんな味かと。
私は答えるだろう。
それは　何ものにも

たとえがたい　と。

マランチャへ向かう途中の
水田で
私たちは車を降りて
ガブリッチ神父が亡くなった場所で
祈りを捧げた
彼の禁欲的な魂のために。

クロアチア語で私が唱える「我らが父」と
英語で彼らが唱える「我らが父」が対面する。
黒い川と白い川が
互いに注ぎ込み
二本の剣が
互いの鞘に収まる。

路上の我ら三人は
人の為すことの
深遠に迷い込み
途方に暮れて立ちつくす。

水田に流れ込んだ血
紅茶に注がれたひとの乳
天国の魂。

訳注　アンテ・ガブリッチ神父はマザー・テレサの友人。

一九九七年十二月十四日．西ベンガルにて

レイモンド・カーヴァーの指輪

一九八八年から八九年にかけての冬
私はレイモンド・カーヴァーの指輪を嵌めていた。
四角い半貴石がついた指輪。ムーンストーンだと
彼の未亡人テス・ギャラガーは言った。
春になる前に　私はその重たい指輪を左手から外し
書き物机の引き出しの中にしまった。
雪もまだ解けきらぬ頃　一通の手紙がテスから届く。
もしかすると　あなたはもうあの指輪を嵌めてないんじゃないかしら？

それならどうかわたしのもとへ　ワシントン州 天使の港(ポート・アンジェルス)へ送り返していただきたいの。

ムーンストーンの指輪を箱に収めてしまう前に
私はその深緑色の滑らかな表面を指先で触りながら
神と天使たちに呼びかけた。
どうか　安らぎのもたらされんことを
私には重たすぎたこの指輪を　かつて身につけていた人に　またその未亡
　人に
そして私にも。

はたして今　テスは嵌めているのだろうか　カーヴァーの重たい指輪を。
あるいは彼女もまた　自分の書き物机の引き出しか
金庫の中にしまっているのかもしれない。

私に分かっていることはただ　それが重たい指輪だったこと。
シルバーの台座に嵌めこまれた四角いムーンストーン。
それを身につける者に　変化を引き起こし　想像力を奮い立たせ
そしておそらくは　狂おしさに駆り立てる。

カーヴァーの指輪から解放された後も
私はたくさんの詩を書いた。
指輪を嵌めていた頃書いたものと
それらは何も違わない気がするけれど・・・。

太平洋の岸辺で眠るレイモンド・カーヴァーよ　永遠なれ
そして　かつてテスが語ったように
ファン・デ・フカの海を眺めながら
その目で鮭の鰭を追い続けるがよい。

なんと幸せな 愛すべきフィッシャーマンだったことか

レイ・カーヴァー。

一九九八年七月十八日 ブラチ島セルカにて

環

わたしは詩人ではない
わたしはわたしではない
わたしは医者ではないし
賢者ではない
わたしは子どもでも
大使でもない
わたしはただ

鼓動を刻む心臓

そして　脈を取る

たなごころ

一九九九年十一月二十日　アレクサンドリア～カイロ間の列車にて

クレオパトラの毒蛇

その蛇が　はたしてこの地であなたを噛んだかどうかなど
あなたの人生の物語にとって　どうでもいいことだ
しかし　イスケンデルンの海辺で
潮風の中に佇む　私の午後にとっては
大問題。

私を噛む　爽やかな海風
——真珠の牙でできた
クレオパトラの毒蛇。

さて　どうしたものか
このスラヴの血潮を流れる毒
わが心臓を内も外も覆い固めている
どこで　どうやって　解毒しよう
いかにして　いかなる目的で　使い果たせばよいのだ
一滴　また一滴
己が血を　熱きローマ風呂の中に滴らせながら
やがて　深い闇に沈み
慈愛に満ちた腕の中へ身を委ねる
額を逸れて　唇に舞い降りた接吻。

二〇〇〇年四月十七日　イスケンデルン／アレクサンドリアにて

輪廻転生(メテムシコーシス)

ガラスの森で肉体が朽ちるとき
息を深く吐き出した墓地の上に　魂の群が立ちのぼり
藁でできた一羽の鷲を白く飾る。

炎が水中に燃えさかり　渦を巻いて舞い上がる土埃。
わたしは最期の時の彼方へと　探しさすらう
ああ　白き魂よ　お前の翼は何処(いずこ)に？

絶壁

彼は気づいた、
握っているのは　死神の手だった、と。
巨大なハサミを持つ　一匹の蟹が
ひくひくと　不器用そうに
彼の心臓をつかんでいるようだった。

夜のガスパール

あなたは夜通し眠っていた。
テーブルに脱ぎ散らかした
衣の波間に
光の消えた星々が　ころがっている。
鼻腔と涙管の交わる角に溜まった
白い涙の粒。

そよ風が　そっとノックしても

あなたは　瞼を開かないだろう。

ハート型の魚

あなたは鷲
わたしのハートを掴んで　太陽へと羽ばたいて行く。
長い歳月　わたしは　一粒のダイヤモンドを磨いてきた
嘆きもせず　それを重荷ともせずに。
力強き鷲よ、抱擁の宿り、
あなたは　友にして　恋人
その瞳の輝きを　胸の中に吸い込み

ゆるやかな翼の愛撫でこの身を癒し　わが力に変えよう。

無常の海の岸辺に
わたしは今、すべての言葉を
着物のように脱ぎ捨てた
――生まれたままの姿となって
子どものように無防備に
あなたの中へと入ってゆく。

畢竟　波のはるか上に輝く　一粒の光。

天の底
ナディール

揺るぎなき星々に錨を下ろした　光の船をめざして
わたしはよじ登っていった。
おどおどとしたナイフ捌きで
炭色に沈む太古の森から　ロープを切り離す。
軽やかな波に乗って　はるか沖へと漕ぎ出してゆくわたしの船。
風の翼で波を切り
やがて　深い海の底へと沈みながら

わたしは蒼き獣を　黄金に鍛えた。

ターニング・ポイント

あなたを殺す刃はまた
あなたを救いもする。

広漠とひろがる暗い地の底に
とんでもない大風が目覚めるものだ。

目を閉じたら
稲妻が空を切り裂くその光景を
見逃してしまうことになるのだよ。

ZEPHYR（そよかぜ）

もし 二山のパンを持っているなら
一つを貧しき者に与え
残りの一つは売ってしまうがよい。
そうして ジャスミンの花をお買いなさい
あなたの 魂(こころ)を満たすために。

日本の絵はがき

カズオ・イシグロに捧ぐ

神奈川にも　やはり　海があるのだね
打ち寄せる波に導かれ　僕らは巡り合い
互いに見知らぬ国から漕ぎ出でた小舟たちが
波のまにまに行き交う

神奈川でも　やはり　富士山が見えるのだね
雪の帽子を頂く　神の国

黒々とした波の頭に　砕け散る

白く　はかなき飛抹(もの)たち

一九八八年夏、ロンドンにて

ドラゴ・シュタンブクのこと

テス・ギャラガー

一九六一、二年のことだったと思う。私はクロアチア語しか話せない、まるで言語の孤島のような或る高齢の婦人のもとに滞在した。彼女は私の未来の夫となる人の祖母だった。会うに際して、彼は私にこう警告した。「いいかい、おばあちゃんが何と言おうと、ただイエスと答えているように。もしノーと言ったら、ぼくらが説明しなくちゃならなくなるからね」と。私はこの条件を受け容れた。彼女のことがちょっと恐ろしかったのだ。稲妻のような激しさが彼女にはあった。稲妻との和平協定。落雷死、落雷火事は起こさない、ただし、有効期間は当座の間とする！　だが、そんな風に怯えながらも、同時に、忘れ去られた孤島のような彼女の風情にたちまち心引き寄せられてゆく自分がいた。私にとって、クロアチア語とは「内に No を秘めた Yes の言語」となった。口にすることのできない No に縁取られた神秘の「Yes」の島。

私の最初の夫は、クロアチア人とアイルランド人のハーフだった。私にもアイルランド系の血が流れているので、彼のアイルランドの遺伝子とうまく寄り添ったのだろう。私たちは十年間をともにしたが、そのうちの何年かはヴェトナム戦争に奪われた。夫は戦時中、大尉として海兵隊のジェット機を操縦し、機銃掃射やナパーム弾投下を行い、かの地に甚大な被害を与えた。彼自身、そのことを決して立ち直ることはできなかった。結婚生活が終わる時、私は彼の苗字を永遠に持ち続けると約束した。そして、いまもそれを守っている。ギャラガーという名は私のすべての詩に記され、そしてまた、ギャラガー家には私自身も知らない神秘的なクロアチア系のアイデンティティーが宿っていたのだが、どうやら私はその謎をもしっかりとこの腕に抱き続けてきたらしい。

　そのことを実感したのは、一九八四年にロンドンのドリス・レッシング邸のガーデンパーティーで、ドラゴ・シュタンブクと私がロンドンに出会ったときだった。レイ［＝三番目の夫レイモンド・カーヴァー］と私がロンドンを訪れた際、すでにオーストラリアでレイと面識のあったレッシング女史は、多くの友人を招き、私たち二人に引き合わせて下さった。その中の一人にドラゴがいた。不思議なことに、互いの手を取り合った瞬間、私はずっと前から彼のことを知っていたような感じにとらわれた。この種の

感覚というのは説明のしようがない。天から授かった友情とでも言おうか。離ればなれになっていた旧知の二人が、今ようやく取り戻せた絆の再開、というような。ドラゴと私は、森の中で焚き火を焚いて暖を取る二人の子どものように、打ちとけ合い心を開いて語り合うことができた。それは弾けるように楽しい思い出だ。私たちはよく散歩に出掛けたりおしゃべりをした。初めのうちこそ照れていたレイも、私と一緒にドラゴとのつき合いを心から楽しんでいた。ある時、彼にドラゴの訳詩を何編か読んであげたことがある。詩心を持ち、散文に勝るとも劣らぬほど詩を愛していたレイが、感動のあまりこう叫んだのを覚えている。「こりゃ、ほんものの詩人だ！」

レイはクロアチアに起こった戦争を知らずに亡くなった。ヴコヴァルの爆撃を嘆き悲しんで書いた自作の詩を歌うドラゴの歌声も聞くことはなかった。爆音が響くさなか、ドラゴは受話器の向こうから切々と私にその歌を歌ってくれた。彼の祖国とそこに生きる人々に対する痛切な思いが突き刺すように私にも伝わってきた。彼はさまざまなことを私に語った。戦争の恐怖というものの内側を。そうした痛みを通して私たちはいっそう絆を強くした。ドラゴが最初の駐英クロアチア大使となったとき、私は難民救済の義援金を送った。クロアチアが独立国家として認められる

72

には、ある種の政治力がそれを支えねばならない。アメリカはその一つだった。私は我が国の上院下院の議員たちに手紙を書いたり電話を掛けて動き始め、最終的には嘆願書の発起人となった。ロバート・ハースやチェスラフ・ミウォシュといった影響力のある作家をはじめ、多くの人々が署名をしてくれた。私はこの嘆願書を上下両院へ送った。スロベニア共和国の例と比べれば、クロアチア承認の過程は信じられぬほど遅々として消極的なものであったけれど、私のささやかな努力も少しはその役に立ったと信じたい。

　エジプト駐在大使の任期を終えてクロアチアに帰国したドラゴに、ある時私はこんな提案をした。このたびのことでクロアチア各地にはさまざまな不和や傷が残されてしまったでしょう。それらを癒してくれるような公園を国内に作ったらどうかしら？　誰もがやってきて庭造りに参加できる、腰を下ろしては木々や水、花や石とともに時を過ごせる、そんな場所、平和の庭。それはあくまで私の夢だ。実現する日が来るかどうかわからない。けれど、少なくともその時私は提案し、私たちは二人してしばしそのことを思い描いた。友達とは、つまるところまさにそのためにいるのではないだろうか。一緒に大事なことを夢想することのできる存在。彼がいなければ、作家としても一個人としても、私はこれほどに多くの恵みを授かることはなかっ

たろう。

何年か前、ドラゴの英訳詩を数編、文芸誌「プラウシェアズ」に掲載させてもらう機会があった。その際、私は次のような紹介文を書いた。

かつてカナダのヴァンクーヴァーで、ドラゴがクロアチア移民の聴衆に向かって詩を朗読するのを聞いたことがある。その声はじつに優しい響きをしていた。まるで森の空き地で語りかけているかのような、神秘と野生と美に包まれ、それでいて安らぎを与えてくれる声だった。私がむかし彼に言ったことは、やはり正しかったのだ。
「今わの際、あなたに枕元で看取ってもらえたらいいでしょうにね。そしてクロアチア語で詩を朗読してもらえたら……」と。

ドラゴの詩は謎に満ちている。けっして澄み渡る水のようではない。しかし、読んだ者に渇望を与える。生の、魂の、そして彼の詩がみずから具現化して見せてくれる人生の、燃えるような激しさに対して、人は渇えを覚えるはずだ。いうなれば、それは暗闇によって活性化する井戸水のようである。上も下もまったき闇に包まれ、彼の詩は我々読者がその深遠へ辿りつくことで蘇るのだ。今の時代、時として人は、

優しさを抑制せよと求められているように感じることがある。だからこそ、あなたの心の中に咲くあの庭を思う存分咲かせるがいいと言ってくれる人、あの優しさの庭を踏みにじらない人に出会えると、心から感謝したくなる。私にとって、ドラゴ・シュタンブクとはまさにそんな人なのだ。彼の存在、彼の詩、すべてにおいて、人の優しさに満ち溢れている。優しさを人に与え、また人から受け取ることのできる人。ドラゴと出会えた私は、詩人としても人間としても、本当に幸せ者だと思う。

謝辞

本書の刊行を実現してくださった次の方々に感謝を捧げる。日本ペンクラブ、宮川慶子、白石かずこ、村上春樹、テス・ギャラガー、ヴィパン・シャーマ、トミスラフ・ブンタク、ミコ・マエダ。そして、とりわけ橋本博美とアイーダ・ヴィダン。二人の翻訳がなければ、この本は存在しなかった。

D. S.

ドラゴ・シュタンブク略歴

 ドラゴ・シュタンブクは、クロアチア共和国ブラチ島のセルカで一九五〇年に生まれた。一九七四年、ザグレブの医科大学を卒業し、その後さらにザグレブ臨床医学センターにて内科を専攻し、併せて消化器病学、肝臓学を研究。一九八三年から一九九四年までロンドンに在住し、肝臓病の科学的臨床的研究とAIDSの実験的治療に従事した。一九九一年から一九九五年まで駐英クロアチア外交代表、また一九九五年から二〇〇〇年の間に、インド、スリランカ、エジプト、スーダン、ヨルダン、クェート、レバノン、カタール、イエメンなど多数の国のクロアチア大使を歴任する。二〇〇一年から二〇〇二年まで、ハーバード大学特別研究員。二〇〇五年から駐日クロアチア全権大使を務める。

 一方で、一九七三年より創作活動を始め、すでに三十三冊にのぼる詩集や評論がクロアチア語、英語、フランス語、アルバニア語、アラビア語で出版されている。また、彼の作品はクロアチア現代詩の重要なアンソロジーに多く収められ、母国をはじめ海外でも数々の文学賞を受賞している。つい先頃、クロアチア科学芸術アカデミーより、もっとも権威あるドラグティン・タヂヤノヴィチ賞(二〇〇八年度)を授与された。

About the Author

Drago Štambuk was born in 1950, on the Island of Brač, Croatia. He graduated from Medical School in Zagreb in 1974 and went on to specialize in internal medicine with sub-specializations in gastroenterology and hepatology at the Clinical Medical Center in Zagreb. From 1983 to 1994 he lived in London where he conducted scientific and clinical research on liver diseases and experimental treatments of AIDS. Between 1995 and 2000 he served as the Croatian ambassador to various countries, including India, Sri Lanka, Egypt, Sudan, Jordan, Kuwait, Lebanon, Qatar and Yemen. He was a Fellow at Harvard University in 2001-2002 and from 2005 has continued his diplomatic service as the Croatian ambassador to Japan. His writing career spans from 1973 and includes 33 collections of poetry in Croatian, English, French, and Spanish. His work has been included in all relevant anthologies of Croatian contemporary poetry. He has received numerous literary awards in his native country and abroad. He is the first receipient of Dragutin Tadijanovič Awards established in 2008 by the Croatian Academy of Sciences and Arts.

Acknowledgement

For making this book possible my gratitude goes to Japanese PEN and Keiko Miyakawa; Kazuko Shiraishi, Haruki Murakami and Tess Gallagher; Vipan Sharma, Tomislav Buntak and Miko Maeda. Above all to Hiromi Hashimoto and Aida Vidan without whose translations the book would not be here.

D. S.

give evidence. They are like well water, refreshed by darkness, a round darkness above and below, refreshed by our reaching toward them. At times it seems as if the world wants to hold us back from tenderness. This makes one thankful for every person who allows that garden in us to bloom, who doesn't trample that garden of tenderness. Drago Štambuk is for me just this person, both in his being and in his poetry, who allows a plentitude of human tenderness—who gives it and is able to receive it. I am the luckiest of poets and of persons to have met him.

Tess Gallagher
December, 2004

writers signed—among them Robert Haas and Czeslaw Milosz. But many others. I sent this petition to Congress and to the Senate. This process was unbelievably slow and reluctant as compared to Slovenian recognition. I believe my efforts may have helped in a small way.

I recall saying to Drago once after he returned to Croatia from his post as Ambassador to Egypt: why don't you make a garden in Croatia dedicated to healing differences and wounds from this time? Everyone could come together to make it. A place to sit and be with trees and water and flowers and stones. My dream: a peace-garden. I don't know if it will ever happen, but at least I could suggest it and we could imagine it for a moment together: that's what friends are for, after all, being able to imagine important things together.

I once had the privilege to publish some English translations of Drago's poems in an issue of Ploughshares. I introduced them this way: "Once I heard Drago read to a Croatian immigrant audience in Vancouver, Canada. It was so tender, the timbre of his voice, that it was as if he were speaking to the listeners in a clearing in the woods, surrounded by mystery and wildness and beauty, but giving them comfort too. That's why it's true I said to him that I wished he could be at my bedside when I'm dying: to read those poems in Croatian."

Drago's poetry is mysterious. It is not clear as water. But it makes you thirst for the intensities of life, of spirit and embodied life of which poems

Australia and she had gathered many of her friends to meet us. Drago was one of these friends. It was strangely as if I'd always known him when we took each other's hands. Who can account for these things? The gift of friendship that seems to be taking up of some closeness we have always known, but been separated from and now regain. He and I could speak in the most frank, open way—like two children building a bonfire in the forest to keep warm. I remember so many exuberant walks and talks—some with Raymond Carver who was my husband by then and with me when Drago and I met. Ray was shy at first, but he too loved to be Drago's company with me. I read some translations of Drago's poems to Ray once and I recall how impressed he was, for he had an instinct about poetry and loved it really more than prose. "He's a real poet!" Ray exclaimed of Drago.

     Ray did not live to know about the war brought about in Croatia. He did not hear Drago singing the song he'd written to mourn the bombing of Vukovar—singing it to me heartbreakingly on the telephone while the bombing was still going on. In that song I could feel acutely his pain for this place and its people. He told me things, the inside of certain horrors of war, and I became more connected through those pains. I sent money for refugees when Drago became the first Croatian Ambassador to England. Before Croatia could get its stature as a separate country again, certain powers had to support that. One of those was America. I began to write and call my congressmen and senators. Ultimately I constructed a petition which many important

Afterword

In 1961 or 62 I met a small island of Croatian language lodged in a very old woman, the grandmother of my husband-to-be. When I met her, he warned me: whatever she says, just say yes. If you say no, we'll have to explain. I accepted these terms of meeting because she made me a little afraid. She was intense like a bolt of lightning that had made a pact not to burn anything down or strike anyone dead—for the moment at least! At the same time she seemed lost, isolated and my heart went out to her immediately, despite my fear of her. Croatian became for me the language of YES with a secret NO inside it. A mysterious island of "yes" fringed with the unsayable NO. My husband-to-be was half Croatian and half Irish. Since I am part Irish I connected very well with this Irish part. We were together ten years, part of which was given over to the Vietnam War in which my husband was a Captain who flew jets in the Marine Corps, strafing and napalming and doing so much damage which he hated, that he never recovered from. When my marriage ended, I promised to keep his name forever. And so I have. The name "Gallagher" is on all my poems and inside the Gallagher is a mysterious unknown Croatian identity that I nonetheless also have kept tight in my grasp.

This "keeping" became possible when I met Drago Štambuk in London at Doris Lessing's garden party in 1984. Ray had met Ms. Lessing in

A Japanese Postcard

(Kazuo Ishiguro)

In Kanagawa there is still the sea,
confluent waves that make us meet,

and long boats that cross paths
with boats from other spheres.

There is still a sight of Fuji,
the snowy cap of God's lands,

and fragile white-headed beings
in the summit of dark waves.

London, summer 1988.

Zephyr

If you have two loaves of bread
give one to a poor man,

sell the other
and buy jasmine
to feed your soul.

Turning Point

The knife that kills
will also save you.

Where the dark abyss extends
the tall wind awakens.

If you close your eyes
you will miss the sight
as the lightning strikes.

Nadir

I climb towards the bright boat
anchored to the firm stars.

I cut the rope with a timid knife
from a charcoal ancient forest.

And I sail away along the light wave
smashing against the wings of wind.

Into the depths of the sea I sink,
forging the blue beast in gold.

unprotected like a child.
The end is a light above waves.

Heart-shaped Fish

You are an eagle carrying
my heart towards the Sun.

A diamond I've been polishing
for years—without heaviness or lament.

You powerful eagle, a home of embraces
a friend and lover, breathe in

the brightness of your eye and ease
of slow strokes into my efforts.

After I left all my
words, like clothes,

on the shores of the ever changing sea
naked I enter You,

Gaspard

You slept through the night.

Extinguished stars are lying on the table,
over the scattered clothes.

In the naso-lachrymal corners
white grainy tears.

Breeze knocking on the eyelids.
You will not open.

Cliff

In his hand
he recognized the hand of death
and he felt as if a crab,
spasmodic and awkward
with enormous pincers,
was clutching his heart.

Metempsychosis

When the body decays in a forest of glass
the swarms rise above the breathed-out cemetery;
dressing a straw eagle in white.

Fire in water, the dust upward swirls.
I search beyond the last hours;
where, o white soul, where are your wings?

sinking into the darkness, in merciful
arms, kissed by mistake
on the lips instead of forehead.

                              Iskendria/Alexandria, April 17, 2000

Cleopatra's Asp

Whether the snake bit you here
matters nothing for your story,
but for my afternoon in the wind
by the sea in Iskendria
it matters.

Bite the fresh sailing sea wind
—Cleopatra's asps were made
out of pearly teeth.

And what will I do with the venom
in Slavic veins
and in my heart coated with it
from within; where, how
can I get rid of it—how and with which
purpose use it up
while I release
drop by drop, my blood
in the hot Roman baths—

Cirle

I am not a poet.
I am not me.

I am not a doctor
or a wise man.

I am neither a child
nor an ambassador.

I am a heart
which beats

and a hand which
feels the pulse.

Alexandria-Cairo,
On the train, November 20, 1999.

What a happy and beloved fisherman he was, Ray Carver.

Selca on Brač, July 18, 1998

widow, and to me, for whom the ring was too heavy.

Whether Tess wears it now, Carver's heavy ring,
or whether she put it in the drawer of her
writing desk, or even in a safe, I don't know.

I do know that it was a heavy ring, a square-shaped
moonstone cast in silver, and that it inspires
changes, strengthens imagination, and maybe causes madness.

Freed from Carver's ring, I wrote
many poems which I cannot differentiate
in any respect from the poems I wrote
during the time I wore it.

Long live Raymond Carver,
who lies on the shores of the Pacific
and, as Tess said, watches the Strait of
Juan de Fuca, resting
his eyes on the fins of salmon.

Raymond Carver's Ring

The entire winter of 1988/89 I wore Raymond Carver's
ring. A ring with a square
semi-precious stone. Moonstone,
his widow Tess Gallagher called it.

Before spring I took the heavy ring from my left hand
and put it into the drawer of my writing desk.

Not much snow had melted when
a letter arrived in which Tess, suspecting I no longer
wore the ring, asked me to send it
back to her to Port Angeles, Washington State.

Before I packed the moonstone ring
into a box, I touched its dark green
smooth surface with my fingertips and
called out to God and the angels: that they should bring
peace to the one who used to wear it, to his

for his ascetic
soul.

My Our Father in Croatian
faced their Our Father in English.
A black and white river
that flow into one another,
knives that pierce
each other's sheathes.

The three of us on the road
lost in our quest
for man's inscrutable
deeds.

Blood in the rice fields,
human milk in tea,
a soul in heaven.

West Bengal, December 14, 1997

Beautiful Woman of Bengal

Beautiful woman of Bengal,
sorrow crushed me
as you expressed milk
from your breast
for the tea of a passerby.

They will ask me back home
about the taste of tea
with human milk
and I will tell them
that such tea is
incomparable to any
other.

In the rice fields
on the way to Malancha
we stepped out of our car
at the site of Gabrić's death
to say a prayer

Language of a Blade

I hid myself, buried by one accidental and discarded word
into the scar of memory.
I curled up, twisted, and wrapped underneath
like my mother's folded linens on the table.
I burrowed myself into the brain's tightest fold.

I still have not unfurled in the northern wind
wrapped in checkered flag.
We have gambled away a thousand and one opportunities,
have built a house of trouble, a state of incessant sighs,
in the ultimate ravine, in a void filled with a whisker of sea.

And you, do you grin, do you toss ripe apples
out of square-shaped cities, my dear, pretending they are wormy?
Checkmate is a reason for unimportant happiness,
a key to an open door.

Cinnamon, Rugged Mountain

We crossed the sea of wild words
and brought glassy silence to our hearts.
With one glance we took in everything
(mountain and sea), reducing it
to a white burning point.   All hearts,
our own and others', we compressed into a magic
rug—so it can carry us to the mountains
and clouds, to the highlanders, into the temple.

The unconsumed coffee at "The Hague"
and the wrist fair as a child's face
will follow me until the end of the world.
Because of his wrist and tenderness, his clumsy
step, because of Bosnia and affection.
The people who give from their softest
and deepest essence, the skin of an angel.

Vienna, Schottengasse, March 11, 2005.

and having shaken it I said:
"These hands are holy."

He excused himself saying
that his boss may get angry
if he finds him sipping coffee in "The Hague.

He managed to say that he was from Rudo,
his wife from Sarajevo, that he had two
kids: Hamid and Benjamin,
that he was 35 although he appeared
much older.

I met Muhamed from the heart of Bosnia
in the center of Vienna,
with whitened hands
and attire. For a handshake
he stretched his wrist, delicate
pale skin untouched
by mortar, the spot where the pulse is palpable
and measurable, where the blood
strikes coming and going to life.

The Wrist

In the café "The Hague" I didn't have coffee
with Muhamed from Bosnia.
He shyly offered his wrist
instead of hand
since his palms were
dirty with lime.

He works in a Benedictine cloister
next to the exhibit of Leonardo's inventions,
which sanctify the human mind and strengthen imagination.

I recognized him by his slow
Bosnian step and unkempt
work attire, sprinkled with white
as if he were a worker-angel.

I accepted the offered
wrist, but immediately
I took his whitened hand

Think good and do good.
You will become God
when in the souls of others
you recognize your own.

My son and my God.

Drown the word in your own mind,
shed your body and discard it.
Do not lose or scatter yourself along the way.
Out of sand fuse yellow gold.

My son and my God.

Do not look for the vices of others.
Look for your own and correct them.
Mercy is in a small bottle
with no expiration date.

My son and my God.

Truth needs to be stripped
if you want to understand it.
To our eyes the Lord is visible.
We are a drop that remembers the sea.

My son and my God.

My Father is Paving the Sanctuary

Do not pick green fruit,
let it ripen.
Have patience
with the planted seed.

My son and my God.

The tree does not eat of its fruit
nor does the river drink of its water.
The sword is not for a child's hand
nor is a pen for a warrior's fist.

My son and my God.

Death is a return
to one's only home.
Where life sprouts
darkness already lives.

Black Widow

I saw a black widow on the island of Brač. Biology professor
Dominik Vlahinić caught it and placed in a glass container.
It had long black legs, a black back with red
spots, black head and a long black fang for injecting
venom into the victim's body.
I shudder at the thought that I might find it
under my pillow. My face darkens with horror,
my lips elongate into a dolphin's snout.
A thousand Adriatic seas could not dilute
this sensation of sharpening.

Poems are sea foam. Spiders live in the lee-side
and the black widow with its red-spotted black back
reigns above the world's sky. Its beauty
is incomprehensible, more demanding
than that of any angel. God is my witness
that I stood, contrite and small, before the glass container.
I was a moist silver of wood, a splinter in a forest of stars.

an unexpected task, his jealous beloved.

She has been waiting for him like this all afternoon,
in her attic room, while her breath
freezes on the window panes and mirrors.

It is getting dark already,
lights are coming on
in Marul Square,
sinter is howling, and she, as always,
stands by the window and waits.

Split, December, 1986.

Step Out

By a tightly closed window
a soul stands and watches.

Wind cuts
through the cracked panes
moving the heavy curtains.

The soul stares at an empty square,
at paper bags flitting
from one side to another.

Three o'clock sounded long ago.
Perhaps he stopped by
a bookshop window?

Knowing how sensitive he is to cold,
the biting gusts would make him hurry.

Perhaps his mother delayed him,

Jonah

Asleep in the innards of the ship
we will be swept by a storm
and buried in the deep sea.

And we will not even know from where
the storm came, or why our end is such.

What will we, I ask in despair,
see in our dream—while the tempestuous wind
thrusts us deeper and deeper
into the torrential waterfall, dark sea.

Dragon Island

per Ombretta de Stambucco

Tonight the clouds are devouring the Moon, their purple
fingers breaking its silver face into pieces of bready
forgetfulness.　The Godly—from the melancholic rings
on the borders of incomplete worlds—is torn
by wolves with singed fur, while the alloy
of light sprinkles the Brač peaks and turns
the animals' nocturnal traces into a mortal rattle.

Selca, August 1983.

Hermit

Thus we live our days eternal
in a golden ring.

All is in it.   Patient love,
convoluted thought, the knot of yearning.

goat skin cover, chalice, fire.

Beginning and end
joined in circling.

The oily warmth of circles
busies itself in the eyes of the ring.
In your bony finger, it throbs

1918

The ships sail far
taking our beloved away
to distant foreign lands,
far the ships sail.

Taking away our lives
in trunks with white flour
and barrels of golden oil
to greedy foreign lands.

Far sail the ships
tearing our hearts with their prows;
what to do with their halves
in the distant foreign land?

I will be your name,
your heart, your dream.
And I will be a blue boat
rocking us across the sea.

Beyond this, I will be your isle,
your threshold, your wine.
Your cradle and land,
your inheritance and fear.

I will be whatever you long for—
an impossible pattern, a steep descent.
Vertical rise.   Infinity.
A snowy peak, a golden end.

Whatever you wish—all I will be.
Even if I know my ruin lies there.
The only thing I don't want to be
is what's carried away by a black wave.

New Delhi, January 1995

Black Wave

I want to be your love
I want to be all your labor.
I will be your countenance
and your bitter-cold.

I want to be all your flame
I want to be your ocean cliff.
I will be your mad dash,
your sharp edge.

I want to be your song
and all your pain.
I will be your sea,
your only God.

I want to be your shadow
I want to be your sand dune.
I will be your eye's pupil.
A silver bowl.

Who smells the blood from your wound, night bird?

My beloved from the blue sea,
my beloved from the azure sky.

Do you fly at night, night bird
or do you sadly sing a nocturnal song?

Neither do I fly nor do I sing—
I harken to the sound of blood, drop by drop.
I watch the blood's darkest crimson.

The Song of Crimson

Where does your heart keep court, night bird?

On the rose thorn,
on the rose thorn.

Where does your heart beat, night bird?

Beneath my beloved's window,
beneath my beloved's window.

Where does your heart bleed, night bird?

On the rose thorn,
on the rose thorn.

Where does the blood from your heart flow, night bird?

In the blush of the rose,
in the blush of the rose.

Black Wave

Gaspard   35
Heart-shaped Fish   36
Nadir   38
Turning Point   39
Zephyr   40
A Japanese Postcard   41

Afterword   by Tess Gallagher   42

Acknowledgement   47
About the Author   49

Sponsored by United Ocean Enterprise Ltd.

A Table of Contents

The Song of Crimson   6
Black Wave   8
1918   10
Hermit   11
Dragon Island   12
Jonah   13
Step Out   14
Black Widow   16
My Father is Paving the Sanctuary   17
The Wrist   20
Cinnamon, Rugged Mountain   23
Langage of a Blade   24
Beautiful Woman of Bengal   25
Raymond Carver's Ring   27
Cirle   30
Cleopatra's Asp   31
Metempsychosis   33
Cliff   34

Black Wave

Drago Štambuk
Translated by Aida Vidan

黒い波 *Black Wave*

著者　ドラゴ・シュタンブク　©Drago Štambuk

訳者　アイーダ・ヴィダン（英語訳）　橋本博美（日本語訳）

発行者　小田久郎

発行所　株式会社思潮社
〒一六二-〇八四二　東京都新宿区市谷砂土原町三-十五
電話〇三（三二六七）八一五三（営業）八一四一（編集）

印刷　三報社印刷株式会社

製本　誠製本株式会社

発行日　二〇〇九年三月二十日